KNOWSLEY LIBRARY SERVICE

Knowsl@y Council

Please return this book on or before the date shown below

You may return this book to any Knowsley library
For renewal please telephone
Halewood - 486 4442   Housebound Service - 443 4223
Huyton/Mobile - 443 3734/5   Kirkby - 443 4290/89
Page Moss - 489 9814   Prescot - 426 6449
School Library Service - 443 4202
Stockbridge Village - 480 3925   Whiston - 426 4757
http://www.knowsley.gov.uk/

The Story of Bear

Hilary McKay

Hodder
Children's
Books
A division of Hachette Children's Books

To Phoebe with love from Hilary.

First published in Great Britain in 2007
by Hodder Children's Books

Hodder Children's Books is a division of
Hachette Children's Books

Hodder Children's Books, 338 Euston Road, London NW1 3BH

Hodder Children's Australia, Hachette Children's Books
Level 17/207 West Street, Sydney, NSW 2000

A catalogue record of this book is available
from the British Library.

HB ISBN: 978 0340 94419 6
PB ISBN: 978 0340 93106 6

Typeset in Cochin

Printed and bound in Germany by GGP Media GmbH

The paper and board used in this paperback by Hodder Children's Books are
natural recyclable products made from wood grown in sustainable forests.
The manufacturing processes conform to the environmental
regulations of the country of origin.

Hilary McKay

The Story of Bear

ONE

The Story of Bear

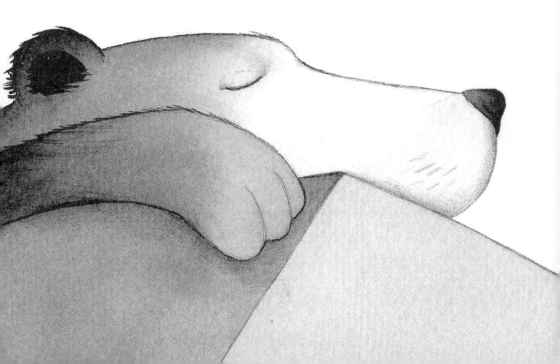

It was Christmas time when the Bear arrived. He was not invited; he just appeared. Nobody needed him.

The Bear was the wrong shape for his wrapping paper, and no way would he fit under the Christmas tree. When he was unwrapped he was too big to be played with properly. Also he was not cuddly. He had a wildish sort of face. They said he looked like he might possibly bite.

"Well," thought the Bear. "I might. Possibly. Bite."

The Bear would not fit beside
the chest of drawers, or in
the cupboard, or on the
windowsill, but they managed
to squash him under the bed.

The Bear stayed under the bed
for several years.

"Just look at him now!" they
exclaimed when they finally pulled
him out. "Awful!"

The Bear was dropped in a skip, face down among the junk with his head buried in cushions and his legs sticking out.

It was winter.

"Awful!" thought the Bear.

The Bear stayed in the skip for

days and days. Sometimes it rained
and the Bear got damp. Sometimes
the sun came out and warmed him.
Sometimes the wind ruffled his fur.

The Bear could not move and
he could not see anything, but he
could feel the sun and rain and
wind.

Also, he felt the parcel of cold fish and chips that was dumped on top of him. And he felt the Seagull who came and ate them up. The Seagull gave the Bear some very good advice as he walked about all over him.

"You want to get a life, mate," said the Seagull.

"Yes, I do," thought the Bear. "I want to get a life."

Children passed the skip on their way from school. They saw the Bear.

"We should rescue him," they said, but they were a bit afraid. They were scared of whoever had put the Bear in the skip.

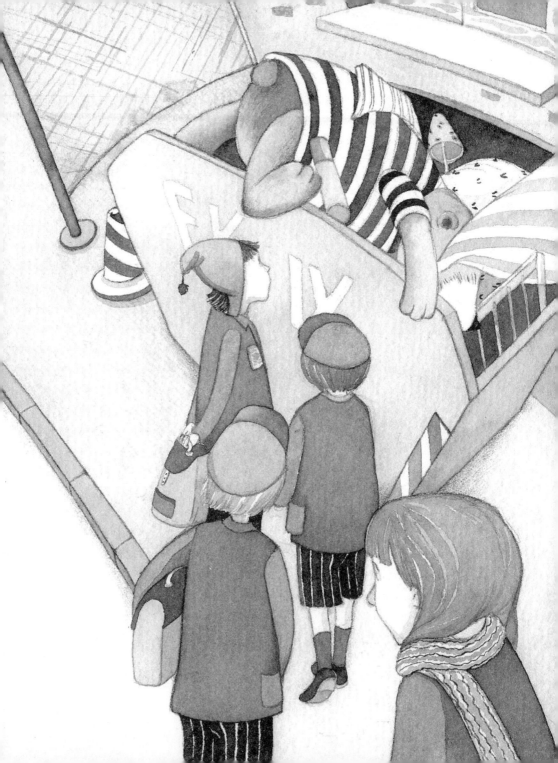

"What kind of person puts a bear into a skip?" they asked each other. "A scary person," they said. "That's what kind!"

Still, in the end, one of them was pushed forward to try. Her name was Ellie and she was smaller than the rest, but braver.

"Go on, Ellie!" they said.

"Go on, Ellie!" thought the Bear.

Ellie tried. She tiptoed up to the skip, reached for a leg, and pulled. The Bear was heavier than Ellie had expected, but that was not the reason why she let go. She squealed, let go, and jumped away. Then she pushed past her friends and ran and ran, right down the hill.

"What's the matter? What's the matter?" panted the other children, pounding after her.

"He felt so strange!" gasped Ellie, rubbing and rubbing the palms of her hands to take that feeling away. "Rough! No. Not rough. Stiff! No, not stiff…"

"Tell us!" said her friends, but Ellie did not tell and the other children soon grew tired of waiting. They started a game of tag in the twilight to warm themselves up.

Ellie looked at her hands. The feeling in her palms was fading fast. It had almost disappeared. She hurried to find the right word before it left her completely.

Real.

"He felt like real!" Ellie called, but her friends were playing their game and they did not hear.

Ellie did not know it, but she had helped the Bear. He was not so squashed. His head was free and he was facing upwards.

Now it was dark.

A pattern of stars prowled across the sky. Another bear. The light from those stars reached the astonished eyes of the Bear in the skip.

It made him blink.

All night the Bear lay and
watched the stars until they faded
and the light came and the sky
turned blue.

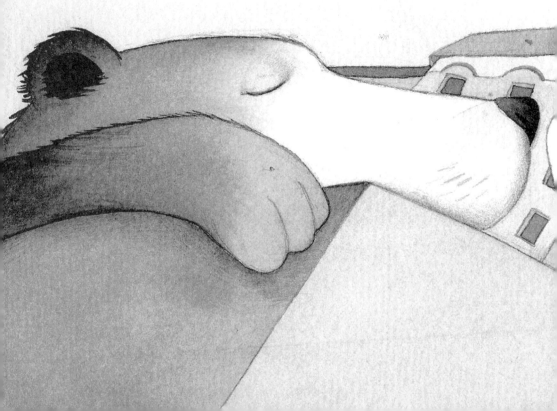

TWO

The Story of Bear

At dawn the Seagull arrived, hoping for more chips for breakfast, which he did not find.

"So this is The Day!" he said, strutting about. "And you've woken up! Teeth! I see, and great big swiping paws with claws attached! Not sure about the whiskers... Whew!"

He leapt into the air. The Bear had tried out one of his great big swiping paws for the very first time and had accidentally nearly beheaded him.

"And you missed, and I'm still alive, so that's good!" continued the Seagull, resettling his feathers.

Then he looked at the Bear. His cold, gold eyes were as wild and amused as the stars had been the night before.

"Now you need a plan!" he said.

"Why do I need a plan?" asked the Bear, arranging his paws on his stomach and looking down his nose at his whiskers. He was very happy with his brand-new view of the sky, and comfy on his cushions. He thought he could stay where he was for ever.

"Mate," said the Seagull, a bit rudely, but not getting too close because the Bear still looked like he might possibly bite, "you've got a long way to go!"

Once again the Seagull was
right. That morning the skip was
taken to the tip. And emptied out.
And levelled smooth. Smoothish,
anyway.

This was the worst thing that had ever happened to the Bear. He smelled smells he did not want to smell, and he saw things he did not want to see. A blue furry ear sticking up from the rubbish like a flag. A rocking horse, trapped.

"Look at them!" moaned the Bear. "Look at this place!"

"It's not so bad," said a voice. "Get over it!"

"Look at me now!"

"I already did," said the voice, and it was the Seagull, gulping his lunch from a torn plastic bag.

"What am I to do? And what is that terrible smell?"

"Someone's nappy," said the Seagull, gobbling away. "Right beside you. Busted open. I should move, mate, if I were you."

The Seagull did not seem a bit sorry for the Bear, and only slightly interested. Still, when he unearthed one of the cushions from the skip, he took the trouble to flip it in the Bear's direction.

"Thank you," said the Bear, and he took the cushion and hugged it tight to his chest and closed his eyes and did not open them again for a long, long time.

Evening came, and the sky turned purple.

Then night, with its patterns of sauntering stars.

Frost cracked in the air, but the Bear did not hear it. Birds called, the morning came. The Bear did not move.

Terrible screaming woke him at last. A terrible screaming voice, the Seagull, beating his wings like a kite caught on a wire, and hopping around with one of his legs trapped in a rusty tuna-fish can. Behind the Seagull was a gigantic bulldozer, roaring closer and closer. It came half hidden in a cloud of dust and it left behind it an enormous flattened silence.

"Fly!" screamed the Seagull.

At last the Bear moved. He dropped his cushion and he jumped to his feet, and he ran. He ran over the mountains of mangled junk. He ran past the rocking horse and the blue furry ear.

Behind him the Seagull called, "Fly! Fly! Fly!"

"Fly yourself!" groaned the Bear.

"Ha!" screamed the Seagull, as amused as ever.

The Bear skidded to a halt
and turned.

Then he charged towards the bulldozer, faster even than he had run before. The dust was so thick he could hardly see, but he could still hear the Seagull.

"Fly!" gasped the Seagull, as the Bear scooped him up from right under the bulldozer's tracks.

The tip where the Bear had been dumped was in the middle of beautiful countryside. All the Bear had to do was run fast enough and far enough. Then push under a wire fence. Then cross a track. And then run some more.

This he did, on three legs, his new enormous paws racing over the ground. His new enormous heart pounding like a drum, and his new enormous whiskers shaking with fear because he was terribly frightened.

"You can stop now, mate," said the Seagull.

They were in the middle of a deep green wood. The ground was hilly and thick with fallen leaves. There was a holly tree bright with berries, and a cave, large and peaceful and empty.

It was totally, completely silent.

The Bear's new claws were exactly what was needed to free the Seagull from the can. After a while the Bear's paws stopped shaking enough to manage this.

Then the Bear crawled into the cave and trembled all night. The Seagull stood guard in the doorway. He stood on one leg because his other was quite sore.

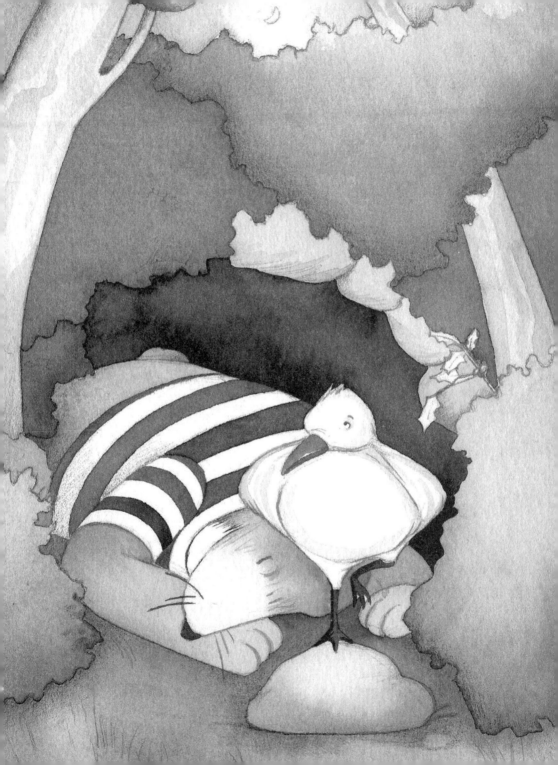

THREE

The Story of Bear

In the morning the Seagull said he was going back to the tip.

"Whatever for?" asked the Bear.

"Breakfast," said the Seagull. "Among other things."

The Bear said he was never going back. Never not ever. He said he was going to live in his lovely cave in the middle of the sweet dark wood.

"Slightly boring, mate," said the Seagull.

The Bear said he would not be bored. He said he  would sleep all day, and watch the stars at night, and live happily ever after.

The Seagull gave him one of his looks and flew off.

The Bear spent most of the day arranging leaves and trying not to think about things too much.

Ellie spent most of the day pestering. She was very sad when she discovered the skip had gone. She knew where skips went.

"To the tip," said Ellie. "I need to go to! I want to see what has happened to that Bear."

Ellie was not only very brave; she was also very stubborn. She cried and argued and pestered until her parents broke down and took her to the tip. They drove into the countryside and parked their car and crossed the track. Ellie's parents held their noses, but Ellie pressed her face against the wire. She did not see the Bear, and this made her hope that he had somehow magically escaped.

However, Ellie did see the rubbish mountains and the bulldozers and the Seagull with the sore leg.

She went home very cross...

The Bear had not enjoyed his leaf arranging. Also he had discovered that he was not very good at not thinking about things too much. Especially rocking horses and blue ears.

The moment the Seagull landed, the Bear hurtled towards him.

"Nice to see you too, mate," said the Seagull, leaping for his life.

"Did you see them?" demanded the Bear. "Are they still there?"

The Seagull kindly did not say, "Thought you were never going back!" Instead he said, "Show you, if you like!" and sailed off at once.

The Bear followed, away from the cave and through the wood and over the track and under the fence and across the rubbish until they came to the trapped rocking horse, and the owner of the blue ear that stuck up like a flag.

"Now, you watch your paws, mate!" said the Seagull. "These people have had a tough enough time already. They don't want squashing flat!"

So, the Bear was very careful as he dug them out, dusted them down and balanced them on their feet – first the rabbit, who washed her face so desperately they thought she would never stop, and then the horse. The horse, finding himself with four free hooves to do what he liked with, leapt in wild dizzy circles around the Bear.

"Off his rocker," said the Seagull, getting hastily out of the way.

"Off his rocker!" said the Bear.

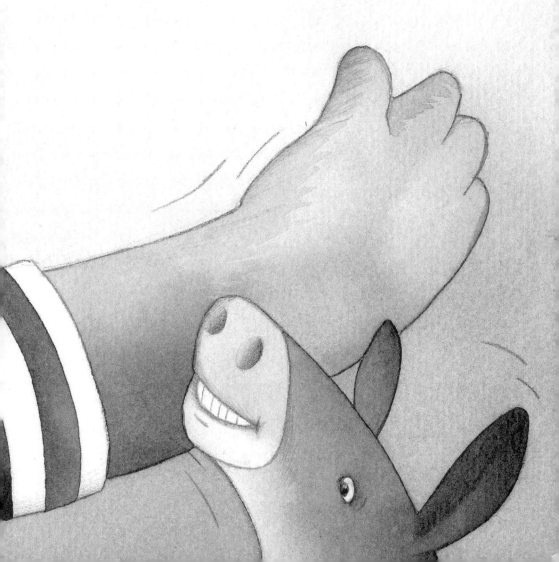

Ellie did not forget the rubbish mountains and the bulldozers and the Seagull with the sore leg.

She did not let her parents forget either.

She told all her friends too.

"I am going to find a better way of doing things than that," she said. And as she was brave and stubborn and hopeful and cross, it was not very long before she did.

Everytime she visited she thought of the Bear. "I'm helping," she told him, silently in her head. "We all are."

The Bear stopped being afraid of the tip. He went there almost every night to pick up the latest arrivals. The Seagull was always with him, keeping watch and offering advice.

"Huff less!" he would say. "You don't want to frighten people. I know you don't bite, but you still look like you might."

The Bear took his advice and was as gentle as possible, considering his size.

"It's not so bad," he would say to each new arrival as he turned them up to the sky. "Look at you! You've woken up!"

"There are woods big enough for all of us very close to here..." the Bear would continue.

"You wouldn't believe what's in those woods, mate!" said the Seagull. "Blue rabbits! Mad horses!"

"...and there is a cave there where you can rest," continued the Bear.

"With cushions!" the Seagull put in. "He's got a lot of cushions. I find them for him."

"You need never come back to this place again... That's right! Up you get! Unless you want to, of course."

"He said he never would," said the Seagull, jerking his head towards the Bear. "He was terrified!"

The Bear huffed with laughter, his warm breath smoking in the frosty air.

"But he got over it..."

The Seagull's cold, gold eyes
gazed proudly at his friend.

"...and just look at him now!"

The Bear tucked the latest arrival under one arm, and then scooped up the Seagull and set him on his shoulder.

"Come," he said happily. "Time to go home."